For the Freedmans – Barry, Steve, Richard and Sally –
and for my long lost cousins Helen and Mary – C.F.

For my grandparents x – S.H.

First published 2015 by Macmillan Children's Books
This edition published 2015 exclusively for Tesco Stores Limited by
Macmillan Children's Books, an imprint of Pan Macmillan
20 New Wharf Road, London N1 9RR
Associated companies throughout the world
www.panmacmillan.com

ISBN: 978-1-5098-0889-2
Illustrations copyright © Tesco Stores Limited 2015
Text copyright © Macmillan Publishers International Limited 2015
Based on an original concept created by Tesco Stores Limited.

1 3 5 7 9 8 6 4 2

A CIP catalogue record for this book is available from the British Library.

Printed in Poland

Written by
Claire Freedman

Illustrated by
Samara Hardy

THE GREAT
CHRISTMAS
PUDDING
RESCUE

MACMILLAN CHILDREN'S BOOKS

Snow fell softly and the air buzzed with excited whispers.
The happy villagers of Pudding Town were watching and waiting
for the Pudding Express train to arrive.

WELCOME TO
PUDDING TOWN

It carried a precious cargo –
all the yummy ingredients needed
for their Christmas pudding festival.

Just then there was a loud announcement.
"DISASTER!" cried the Station Master.
"The Pudding Express is stuck in snow!"

"Oh no!" the people cried. "We can't have our
Great Pudding Festival without it.
What shall we do?"

There was only one thing *to* do.

The children wrote a letter to Santa.

Dear Santa,

The Pudding Express is snowed up at Jam Junction. On board are all the ingredients we need to cook the giant Christmas pudding for our Great Pudding Festival. We can't have a pudding festival without a pudding.

PLEASE HELP!

From,
The People of Pudding Town
X

As the smallest child was about to post the letter,
a sudden breeze blew it high into the frosty sky.

SWOOSH!

Maybe it happened because . . .
They were hoping and caring,
Loving and sharing?

WHEEE! The letter swirled above the roof tops . . .

over the frozen lake . . .

TO: Santa
NORTH POLE

across the forest, and far, far away!

Santa was in his workshop when the envelope
swooped through his letterbox,

looped-the-loop

Dear Santa,

The Pudding Express is
snowed up at Jim Junction.
On board are all the ingredients we
need to cook the great Christmas
pudding for our Great Christmas
We can't have a pudding is
a pudding
PLEASE HELP!

From, People of
The Pudding Town

and landed on his desk.
"Oh dear!" he gasped, reading it.
"Something *must* be done!"

Santa stomped outside into the snow and whistled very loudly!

Out from the trees, animals and birds
came hopping and skipping excitedly.

Santa explained about the train stuck in deep snow.

"What can we do to help?" Squirrel asked.
"I'll show you!" Santa replied.

They followed him into his huge Christmas cavern.
Every shelf was piled high with presents.

"Aha! Found it!" Santa smiled, reaching for a huge cookbook.
"Mrs Claus's very secret Scrumptious Christmas Pudding Recipe.
And here's everything we need to make it!"

There were spicy cinnamon, crunchy almonds, brown sugar, juicy raisins, and sticky treacle. "Delicious!" said Bear, dipping his paw in the treacle.

Santa found fresh brown eggs, creamy butter, squidgy cherries, and zingy ginger.
"Smells lovely!" squeaked Mouse.
"Atchoo!" sneezed Fox, opening the flour packet.

There was even a shiny silver sixpence to
hide in the pudding, and holly to decorate it.
Each of the animals carried off an ingredient.

"Thank you, friends!" said Santa. "I would come with you, but
it's Christmas Eve and I have a *very* important job to do!"

The animals set off for Pudding Town.
But with a few mishaps along the way . . .

They almost got lost in a snow blizzard.
"Follow our singing," chirped the robins. "We'll lead you through!"

Mouse got a little upset when she sat on
some prickly holly that Hare had left behind.
And some cherries went missing!

On the slippery frozen lake, Squirrel dropped her raisins.
They scattered everywhere!

Fortunately Hedgehog was able to collect them in no time.

But they had lots of fun too . . .

Skating across the frozen lake,

egg juggling competitions - oops!

— and snow drift jumping!

"It's getting late," Fox said. "We must hurry!"

At last they saw the twinkling lights of Pudding Town.
"I never thought we'd get here in time," said Rabbit.
"But we did!"

Maybe it was because . . .
They were hoping and caring,
Loving and sharing?

What a surprise the villagers had when they saw the animals bringing such wonderful supplies for their Great Pudding Festival. "Hooray!" they cheered. "Thank you!"

Everyone got straight to work.
There was mixing and stirring,
grating and chopping.

"I'm in charge of the tasting" laughed Bear.
"We're happy to help!" said the children.

There was adding and pouring, measuring and whisking.

Finally the pudding was ready to put in the oven.
"It's almost Christmas!" the people yawned.
"We should get to bed before Santa arrives."

The town awoke to the sound of the robins singing happily.
It was Christmas Day!

Santa had visited overnight and left presents for everyone.

"Snow sledges," laughed the children.

"Raisin cookies!" smiled Hedgehog.

"A giant tub of treacle,"
said Bear with a sticky grin.

In all the fun and excitement they *almost* forgot about their pudding.
Everyone waited with baited breath to see how it had turned out . . .

The pudding was ENORMOUS!
"It's our biggest EVER!" the people cheered.

It was hot and steaming, and the yummy
smell made everyone feel very hungry.
"I can't wait to taste it!" grinned Bear. No one could.

Hooray! It was the best Great Pudding Festival
that Pudding Town had ever held.

The day was filled with feasting and friendship,
sparkles and smiles, singing and dancing.

Best of all, the pudding tasted delicious —
and there was more than enough for all the people and animals.

"Even I can't eat another crumb," Bear sighed.
"We found the silver sixpence!" squeaked the mice happily.

"What a *magical* day we've shared," the villagers said to the animals.
"Thank you for helping us. You saved our Great Pudding Festival!"
The animals smiled.

Maybe it was because . . .
Everyone had been hoping and caring,
Loving and sharing . . .

That together they had all the right ingredients for the perfect Christmas.

And maybe, just maybe . . .
If we begin hoping and caring,
Loving and sharing,
Then our dreams will also come true!